Edward C Caswell

OLD NEW ORLEANS

CLOSED SHUTTERS

The Eighties

By EDWARD LAROCQUE TINKER

LAFCADIO HEARN'S AMERICAN DAYS (1924)

TOUCOUTOU (1928)

(In collaboration with Frances Tinker)

OLD NEW ORLEANS (1931)
    Widows Only (The Sixties)
    Strife (The Seventies)
    Closed Shutters (The Eighties)
    Mardi Gras Masks (The Nineties)

Reprinted from The Century Magazine

OLD NEW ORLEANS

CLOSED SHUTTERS

The Eighties

BY

FRANCES TINKER

AND

EDWARD LAROCQUE TINKER

FRONTISPIECE BY JOSEPH PENNELL

DECORATIONS BY EDWARD C. CASWELL

D. APPLETON AND COMPANY

NEW YORK   LONDON   MCMXXXI

To
JAMES MARTIN McKEE

CLOSED SHUTTERS

The Eighties

CLOSED SHUTTERS

The Eighties.

A THIN-FACED child, dressed in black, with a loaf of bread under her arm, was walking slowly along the brick banquette that ran with a high iron fence on one side and a border of thick tangled grass on the other; beyond it was the wooden edge of a wide gutter full of dark viscous water. As she dawdled on, she shuffled small pebbles and bits of oyster shells that had become lodged in the grass, into the gutter with the toe of her scuffed shoe and listened, apathetically, to the sullen cluck they made as they disappeared, without a ripple, into the thick sluggish muck. The green scum that partially covered it was brilliant and feathery

[3]

and the sun's slanting rays gave it a strange translucence. The pattern it made on the drab, gluey water interested her, so she picked up a little branch of chinaberry tree that she found on the walk and, squatting down by the side of the ditch, poked into it gently, watching the scum rise and fall like velvet in a breeze. It was full summer, and the crêpe-myrtles along the street bobbed their papery blossoms in the light wind that came from the river, only a few blocks away.

She hadn't been there long when a group of little girls came running out of the house behind the high iron fence. Quickly getting up, she turned to watch them, but they disappeared, almost immediately, into the side yard that was not visible from the street. Their laughter brought an answering smile to her little

[4]

face as she craned her neck to get a glimpse of them. But it was useless to try; too many trees and shrubs intervened.

Hunching her bread more closely under her arm, she resumed her listless poking into the gutter. After she had tired of the sluggish swirling of the luminous green velvet, she got up leisurely, threw the muddy chinaberry branch into the middle of the street, and started along absent-mindedly, counting the bars in the tall iron fence. She was touching them as she passed and had gotten to fifteen, sixteen and seventeen, when she stopped abruptly. She had come to the gate with its cross bands and garlands of iron roses. It was heavy and imposing and its lock and bell were ponderous. The gong, as large as her hat, was covered by a shield of heavy netting and, over it, was a little slanting roof to keep it rain-dry.

[5]

As she stood looking around she noticed a pleasant-faced negro mammy asleep on the steps of the square white house with its huge pillars topped with frostings as delicate as those on the wedding cake in the baker's window on Magazine Street.

"May I come in?" she called in a timid, frightened voice. She hardly knew why she wanted to.

The old colored woman opened her eyes with a start. Her head was tied up in a brilliant bandanna handkerchief, and her immense rotundity was almost entirely covered by a white apron whose starched outlines made her look even more shapeless.

"What you say, chile?"

"I say, may I come in?" the little girl repeated, taking courage from Emma's friendly smile.

[6]

"Dey havin' a burthday party." The gay head-handkerchief nodded in the direction of the side yard.

"I wouldn't pester them. I only want to watch—but maybe I'm not fixed-up enough." She glanced quickly at the rusty black dress and the loaf of bread under her arm.

Emma's keen eyes, full of the natural kindness of her race, caught her meaning and, wriggling up slowly and ponderously, like an elephant getting into motion, she shuffled over to the gate.

The child waited; her eyes round and her hands clasped tightly together, while the key in the gate's iron lock turned squeakily and the door to her promised land creaked open. Her shoes were scuffed until the toes were white, and she walked as though she was trying to hide them. As she crossed the red flagging that led to the steps, she turned to look at the children playing "Chickie, ma Chickie, ma Crainie Crow." They were all in fluffy organdies with ribbons flying, and unmindful of everything except their game.

With a little catch in her voice, she sidled up to Emma's blue-ginghamed arm and said softly: "I wouldn't like to play with them. I'd rather sit with you and watch."

After Emma had maneuvered her sitting-down process, which was as complicated as the getting-up one, she asked the child where she stayed and why she had never seen her pass by, "if you lives in my precinc'."

"Oh! I've passed here lots of times, but I never saw anybody out before. My name is Alys Ledoux and I live around the corner on Annunciation, not far from

[8]

Harmony Street. I always go the other way to make market, but today is 'take and get,' and I had more time, so I came around here. I always like it on this block; it's so pretty." She laughed softly. "I'd been standing at the gate a long while before you saw me. I reckon you were taking a nap. You sleep solid, don't you?"

"You sho is right. I don' believe in light-fingerin' anythin', an sleep mos' particular. But what's dat you call 'take an git'?"

Alys laughed easily. "That's nothing nice like Christmas or Easter. It's just the day that my sister and I finish the sewing. She *takes* it back and *gets* more."

"What kind o' sewin' is it?" Emma asked incredulously, looking at the strange little figure beside her. She might have been ten or twelve years old but her eyes looked a thousand.

"It's not dreamy work like embroidering roses or making baby caps; mother used to do *that* before she got sick, but now—we only sew overalls," she answered absentmindedly. She was watching the children at their games, the large ribbon bows on their heads bobbing around like huge butterflies.

The side yard would have made a lovely stage set for a fairy play. The tall board fence at the back was covered by the glistening bignonia vines with their peppering of lavender and yellow blossoms, and on either side, large wind-swayed banana trees rustled their slashed leaves in undulating grace.

Alys watched, as though from a great distance, objects of which she knew little and of whom she felt a strange uneasi-

[10]

ness that almost amounted to fear. "Do they play *all* the time?" she asked presently, almost under her breath, tilting her head in the direction of the children. She found herself wondering how many overalls she could have made while she had been sitting there, and if the little girls in the side yard had been sewing, too, how many *more* overalls they could have made: enough, so that mother would not have to help out when sister was sick and the bundles dwindled slowly.

Emma watched closely the thin face, shiny where the skin pulled over the cheek bones, and the long nervous hands that constantly smoothed her rumpled dress. "Chillun has got to learn to play." Her tone was almost apologetic. She was bewildered by the child's earnest question.

"What's the use of learning that?"

"It keeps em soople."

[11]

"It wouldn't teach them to make over-alls, would it?"

Emma did not answer. Tears came into her eyes as Alys turned slowly and, taking her bread from the step behind her, held out her hand to say good-bye.

"I've got to go now. Mother and sister will be wanting their supper soon. Thank you for letting me in."

"Can't you stay a smidgin longer? Dey goin' have ice cream to reckly."

Alys hesitated a moment; a smile showed her even white teeth. "Ice cream! I'm sure it will be good but—I wouldn't like it much—alone."

"Where 'bouts roun' de corner do you live?" interrupted Emma. "Reckon I can bring you some, later on."

"It isn't far. When you turn down on Annunciation from Harmony, it's the third house; that little gray cottage."

[12]

"De one wid de close shetters?" Emma asked, weighing her words as though, at last, she was solving a mystery which had long puzzled her.

"Yes. We do that for mother. She isn't strong now, and the light hurts her eyes."

Emma watched her open the big iron gate that creaked on its hinges, and close it gently behind her. One glance in the direction of the gay, laughing, birthday party, and the child turned away with no evidence of regret. As she hurried along the street, she waved her thin hand to Emma until she disappeared around the corner.

At her own gate she fumbled absent-mindedly, then remembering the key in her pocket, opened it noiselessly, locking it after her. There was a slight flutter of the shutters at the front window, then

[13]

they were quiet again, as though the watcher was satisfied.

Emma sat for a long time where Alys had left her on the steps of the white house, wondering about the strange child with the dark eyes, so pathetic in her quiet dignity. The old colored woman's intuition told her more than the little girl had, and she patched together the usual story of illness and poverty, but there was something else besides. It baffled her. She was used to ferreting out sensitive secrets, and for years had carried on a sympathetic warfare against privation and unhappiness in the neighborhood. She was "a-servin' o' comfort from de Jedge's bounty," and, as such, was well known all through the poorer sections that surrounded the big square house.

The sinister cottage on Annunciation Street had always given her a creepy feeling, and she had felt hidden eyes peeping at her through the blistered, green shutters when she stopped to look at the huge trumpet vine that densely covered the side porch and hid the back yard from view, its lacquer-red flowers, like so many bells, ready to ring out at a stranger's approach. Once there had been a white lady with dark eyes and a sweet face, standing at the gate when she passed. Her *"Bon jour, tantie,"* had seemed queer in this section of New Orleans where all the people were American. Only a few French families ever lived above Canal Street.

When Emma had asked the fruit-stand man across the way, he said sympathetically that they hadn't been there long. He added that they probably got it cheap enough, as it was in bad repair and had been vacant for some time. "It's just women-folks," he confided, "I reckon they'll be going soon." That was years ago. Since then, Emma had never seen anyone about the yard nor heard anything more. She had even forgotten the details of her conversation with Petucci, and now he had moved away and she did not know where to go for more information.

After the party was over and all the little girls had left, full of ice cream and cake and misgivings as to their ability to handle the load, Emma filled her market-basket with a bountiful supply of the left-overs and a bag of cookies she had made for the next day. She told no one of her errand and started out the side gate, to the little cottage. As she neared it she had the same spooky feeling as though some "evil-minded nigger" had put a *gris-gris* on her doorstep. But Emma had set herself a job to do, and like all the rest of "them onus perdicaments" that

[16]

had come her way since slavery days, she did it with all her might; and with grim determination, she rattled the wooden gate. Almost in frightened terror the shutters on the gallery fluttered and, in a second, Alys came running to the fence.

"I was afraid you'd forget, or be too busy," she said breathlessly.

"No, indeed. It taken me right smart time to travel roun' here, but I brang you yo' sheer o' de party," Emma said smilingly, as she took a bowl of ice cream out of her basket and held it over the square-topped board fence.

"Oh, my! . . . but I can't take it in that beautiful blue bowl."

"You needn' be feared you'll break my tureem. It done stood my reckless method, so I'm sure it safe wid you."

Still the little girl drew back as though afraid to touch it, when a soft low voice from behind the closed shutters, husky as though from a severe cold, said gently:

"Take it, my dear, and thank Tantie."

Emma recognized the voice. The lady who had stood at the gate years before, had not "gone soon," as the old Petucci man had predicted. How lonely it must be for her behind those heavy shutters! Always sewing on overalls and seeing the world through slits of dusty wood. They had once been painted but years had obliterated nearly all traces of it.

Alys took the bowl gingerly, with a frightened look. "Would you mind if you never got it back?" she whispered, staring at Emma with wide open eyes.

"Well . . ." the old woman hesitated, "I wouldn' like it broke for pranciance— but if it was a legal acciden'. . . ."

"I'll do the best I can," Alys interrupted, all the joy gone out of her voice.

[18]

She hastily tucked the bag of cookies under her arm and turned to go.

Mammy watched the little black-dressed figure holding the precious "blue tureem" out in front of her as if it were some sacred vessel to be blessed.

"Dats right, chile; take care is better den beg pardon," and under her breath she added, "Dey got a few clothes over yonder rattlin' roun' us premises, dat jes 'bout fit her. Black no good fo' chillun; dey pores gits full o' sadness soon enough."

She walked home wearily. Her basket weighed heavier on her arm than when it was full. Of all her "neighborin' " visits, this one seemed the most hopeless of satisfying results. She couldn't have told why she was so discouraged, but her mind was "tore up pitiful."

Emma was known throughout the

Garden District as Judge Markham's
"toter" of consolation, and at the first
signs of distress, her bulbous figure, with
its market-basket and brilliant head-
handkerchief, was seen taking out for the
family in trouble. When the problem was
serious she'd call it to "Mister Jimmie"
attention, and generally—although he
was far from being a rich man—a way
would be found to assist those in dire
straits.

Emma loved being bountiful and, when
all her charges were in situations and well
fed, she felt put upon by too much pros-
perity. She knew her type of proba-
tioners, but this new one, little Alys, was
a bit baffling. She could see the poverty
and want, the lack of clothes and good
food, but there was something else she did
not understand. "A veilin' acrost her
sun," she called it.

[20]

At first she carried tid-bits and candies, her quaint humor turning them into offerings instead of gifts; but after a few months Alys confessed to her in whispers that her mother would eat nothing she could prepare. This gave Emma a clue and she began substituting tender chicken for tid-bits, and "risin'-bread" for candies. She knew the impenetrable pride of the Creoles of good family, and in many ways gave them happiness without hurt.

As the months went on and Alys never mentioned the blue tureen, Emma had misgivings of an accident and wished she could ask for the pieces. "Maybe dat white genelman dat glue up de collection plate fo' de Windin' Chapel could do somethin' fo' my tureem." But the little girl looked so frightened and sorrowful every time she saw her, and there seemed something so tragic in the battered tin

[21]

pan that she always brought to the gate, that Emma did not "have de heart" to mention it.

Alys firmly refused to take any dishes or buckets into the house, but insisted that Emma empty her "offerin' " in her pie-tin whose bottom looked like a relief map of the Rocky Mountains.

One day the grocery boy on Magazine Street gave Emma two paper plates for lagniappe when she came in to make her "marketin'." They had just been received and were stacked up on the nearest sugar barrel. At first she looked at them dubiously; she had never seen anything like them before.

"Well," she grunted, "you sho got a tight-fisted generosity, ain't you?" Paper plates had no place in her scheme of things, and she was just getting ready to "res' em permanen' " on the counter and demand her customary soup-bunch as lagniappe, when she thought of Alys's battered pie-plate, and how much more "natural" she could make her "cookins" look if she didn't have to "dump em reckless, like a alley-man gittin' a hand-out over de fence." With a pretense of humility and a sly smile, she asked the boy for two more and waddled off up Magazine Street, nodding her gay *tignoned* head as people spoke to her in passing.

She believed in frank cordiality and consequently admonished her "white chillun" to "bow to people, don't butt at em." She practiced what she preached and there was no mistaking her amiability for animosity.

After her first encounter with paper plates, which she insisted upon calling "Yankee 'conomy," a constant stream of them found their way into her kitchen, and the memory of her blue tureen made her most willing to leave her prized re-membrance-china at home. Even the wine jelly that was sent every week to Mrs. Speed (the family doctor's wife), reposed its amber translucence upon a paper plate.

When Emma first started going to the little house near Harmony Street, she al-ways had to shake the wooden gate several times before Alys would appear; but as the months went by and the cold damp winds began to crumple the trumpet vine and toss the crêpe-myrtle leaves about, she'd find Alys peeping around the back porch, with tear-filled eyes, her thin flut-tering hands ready to clutch the bundle that grew larger and larger each time, and run with it into the house. The gate was never unlocked nor was Emma asked to come into the yard. There was always a great distance between them; a ground of no footprints over which no confidences could travel. Once or twice Alys would squeeze the brown hand, but her gulp of joy and her unshed tears were enough thanks for the good old woman.

THAT winter was an unusual one. Snow in New Orleans was almost unheard of. Stores and schools were closed, and every one who was able was out on the streets grabbing up handfuls of snow and throwing it apologetically at the chance passerby. They didn't seem to know what to do with it. The younger children had never seen it and their joy was not unmixed with fear. The doctors and nurses were busy with unprecedented illness brought on by the extreme cold.

[25]

New Orleans was in a pitiable condition.

Bundles of fat pine and buckets of coal found their way to the house on Annunciation Street. The "take and get" days grew further and further apart and, at last, Emma took counsel with "Mister Jimmie."

"Can't work nothin' out o' this," she grumbled. "Ain' gittin' ahead. Dat poor little Alys look thinner an whiter, an I don't hear dat sewin' machine no mo. Reckon de fact'ry is close."

"Don't be discouraged, Emma, it's too cold for them to sew, and with all the windows down you couldn't hear the machine, anyway. Try putting some money in your bundle. The little girl will keep it if they are in dire necessity. It will take the place of what they can't earn." He handed her a stack of silver dollars from a drawer in his desk.

"Yas sir. You sho is good. I reckon I spends mo of yo' charity money den you does."

"I'm sure you do, and you spend it better. Your hobby's human-beings and mine's books; so we should each stick to the work we know best."

Emma was silent a long time. "I reckon dat not readin' an writin' is good for me," she mumbled, shaking her head slowly.

"Why?" asked the Judge in a quiet, thoughtful voice.

" 'Cause tendin' to live folks is mo better den readin' 'bout dead ones; an Gawd ain' goin' put me out o' Heaven 'cause I can't spell it, is he, Mister Jimmie?"

"You needn't doubt that, Emma. The only fault you'll find with the way God runs things up there is that they will have no poor nor puny, no sick nor sorrowful, for you to worry over." The Judge looked at Emma meditatively. There was a moment's silence.

"Dat's a Hell of a Heaven fo' me," chuckled Emma, waddling toward the door, with her handful of silver cart-wheels jangling in her capacious pocket, her keen sense of humor shaking her round shoulders.

The dreadful weather continued. The water in the gas meters froze. The faucets on all the tall iron-bound cisterns wore long beards of sparkling icicles. The plumbing pipes burst, and the small, flickering fires in the tiny grates paid the empty compliment of cheering without warming. The large base-burner in the hall of the square, white house was kept at red heat all the time, and the fireplaces, with their shallow baskets, were piled high with the smoky, black-oozing, soft

[28]

coal which burned brightly but so quickly that many hodsful were trundled in incessantly. In most of the churches prayers were said for better weather, and in the thin board homes of the poor there was acute suffering. Many people shuffled along with their feet tied up in gunny sacks or layers of the daily papers; and the little bootblacks and newsboys lined their clothes with old issues of the respectable *Times-Democrat* or the scurrilous *Mascot,* whose articles had warmed to bursting heat many a reader when the weather was less inclement and the need was less great. It was serving its only useful purpose now in providing protection against the sneaking, damp, murky cold that sent rigors down one's spine and froze one's very marrow.

Emma's rheumatism had "put her pass" much effort, but on the first day the shame-faced sun struggled through the clouds and stared at the damage its absence had caused, she hobbled up to the bleak, deserted-looking cottage, with her basket full, and black-faced Eddie trailing behind her with a bucket of hot gumbo. He was a short, stocky little negro who had been hired to wait on her in the kitchen and save her steps " 'bout de premises."

Several rattles of the ramshackle gate brought no response. The noise only served to make the silence uglier and emptier.

"Good Lawd!" she ejaculated to Eddie, whose round eyes seemed starting from their black sockets; "Jack Fros' done recked misery roun' here. Reckon de door froze shet."

Several times she shook the gate with the same result. As a last hope she rat-tied it vigorously and was greatly relieved to see a tall, much-bundled-up figure come from the back porch and walk slowly, almost painfully, up the brick walk to the front of the house. Not a feature of her face was visible among the thickly draped wrappings with which she had covered herself. Emma thought it was Alys's mother, and was visibly contrite that she had brought her out in such dreadful weather.

"Please 'scuse me. I'm mighty sorry I shuck de gate so powerful. You better not trust yo'se'f out here in de col'. Sen' yo' little chile for her bunnels, or Eddie can tote em in for you."

"I can take them, mammy. I'm Alys's sister. She couldn't come out again today."

"Has dat chile been plundrin' roun' de street in dis unnatural dampness?" Emma

[31]

asked anxiously. Her sincere concern was very evident.

"She had to help me . . . get mother . . . off." The tall lady's voice was low and weary.

"Where yo' Maw gone? She sho did pick a bad spell o' weather. Ain't you feared she be took wid a worst col' den she been had already?"

"No, mammy, I'm sure she'll be better. She always wanted to go where she could see flowers and butterflies. . . ."

"But where you sen' her?" interrupted Emma. Her eyes were full of tears and she trembled with excitement. The thought of the sick lady going away alone was too much for her.

"California," came the slow answer.

"Good Lawd Jesus! Dat's a awful far piece. Why didn' you sen' fo' me to help you?" she pleaded; "I been stove-up wid de rheumatism an a tetch of de quinsy, but could a-put up a good lunch an' fix her a jug o' water. Dem ice coolers ain' much on a long trip."

Emma remembered the time she had gone to Kansas with the family. It was one of those refugeeing trips to get away from the yellow fever epidemic. When all the many and assorted bundles were put aboard the train, her "jimmyjohn" of water was looked upon with disdain and embarrassment by all members of the family; but when they were going through some of the states that had shotgun quarantine, and the water in the coolers gave out, her demijohn took on great importance and she trundled up and down the Pullman and day-coaches giving the crying children much needed drinks.

"We made her as comfortable as we could. She told me to thank you for

being so kind to my little sister." Miss
Ledoux's husky voice broke upon Emma's
consciousness and she realized with a start
that she still had the basket on her arm.
Setting it down beside her on the banquette, she took out the bundles and laid
them on the top of the fence, mumbling as
she did so: "Can't understan' why you
didn' lemme know."

"I'm sorry, mammy."

"Yo' Maw must a-had right smart time
gettin' on dat ole Jackson ferry to ketch
dat train at Gritny."

"She did. It was very hard." The low
voice was tense and bitter.

"Yas, an dat's a whole block to walk
from de turm-table." Emma reminisced
gently as she recalled the time that she
had crossed on the same ferry boat with
Favorite painted in black on the pilot
house.

[34]

The shrouded figure was taking the bundles from the top of the fence and putting them under her arm. The hot gumbo had been poured into her own tin pail and she stooped to pick it up.

"Yo' Maw must a-went in one o' dem bright yaller coaches wid maroom trimmin' all garnished up wid stars an cressens."

"You've seen them, Emma?"

"Yas mam, I seen em. Dey fix em up like dat jes to make de fool niggers think de Knights o' Pefus or de Odd Fellers was runnin' de railroad. California has a long-away soun', ain't it, Miss?"

"It *is* a long way. You'll come often to see Alys, won't you?" Her voice was muffled and unsteady. "She is sorry not to see you now; I'm sure she's watching from the window."

Emma looked at the shutters. They

[35]

fluttered slightly. She waved a warning hand. "Shet dat winder, chile. You ain' got no right tamperin' wid de elements when dey so misjinted as dey is now. I'm goin' brang you some molasses an tar for dat col' you got."

"Not today, please. Alys has enough. Bring it tomorrow; she'll be better then, and waiting for you." Before Emma could reply, Alys's sister had turned noiselessly and vanished behind the gray, crisp network of empty vines whose leaves had long since crumpled in the hard grip of winter.

The old negro mammy stood for a long time looking at the spot where the figure in black had disappeared. "Sho is funny," she said softly. "Creoles mus' be made wid a diffunt yeast. Dey ain' like no other white-folks I ever seen. Dey don' make *nobody* dey confidence."

[36]

She shook her head gently. The situation was baffling to her. She had been coming here for many months and was forced to admit to herself that she knew nothing more of the inside problem of the little gray cottage than she knew the afternoon of the birthday party when Alys sat with her on the steps. Her errands of mercy were not doing any good, as far as she could see, so she determined to talk to the Judge about it again.

Calling Eddie, she picked up her basket and turned to go, but Eddie was nowhere to be seen. "No-'count nigger!" Emma muttered angrily. "He ain' got de sense of a goober-pea. I bet dat double-toothed son o' Ham think dere's a hoo-doo on dis here place." And she hobbled off with an apprehensive glance over her shoulder.

When the family dinner was finished and the dishes were cleared away, Emma

[37]

sat in the kitchen window, waiting for the light to be lit in the Judge's study. She had not looked at Eddie since she came home. He was growing more and more contrite, and more and more agile and helpful, trying to gain her attention and a word to break the monotony of her emphatic silence. She ignored him completely. Once he nearly upset her in his unexpected eagerness to pick up her "bastin' spoon" that had clattered to the floor, but she bore it all in stony silence. At last he tried to placate her by offering to lock up "evvythin' mortal careful" and help her to her room.

"Help? Help?" she thundered, remembering his flight of the afternoon; "De onlies' helpin' you can do is hangin' by yo' tail in Affica, helpin' yo'se'f to cocoanuts. You ain' useful nowhere else. Eddie, 'fo' Gawd, you is de kind o' nigger dat makes me blieve in segergation, an I'm goin' to tell you right now dat yo' room's better den yo' company, an I wants you to dry up an blow out o' dis kitchen."

Eddie could stand no more. He was about to cry. "Aun' Emma, you ain' right to blame me. Dat house got somethin' wrong in it, an when I seen dat white lady comin' out o' dere, all wrap up like a Christmus presen' wid nothin' showin', not even her hands, my heels itch so to tap de banquette dat I jes *had* to run em up de street to quiet em."

"Sho dat lady was kivvered up, an you was kivvered up too, ain't you? If you had a-had any mo rags on you den you did, it would a-took a bloodhoun' to find yo' body. Dat ain' no legal 'scuse for playin' Judas in forsakement."

"But you knows yo'se'f dat dere's somethin' wrong in dat crunched-up little buildin'."

"Sho dere's somethin' wrong, but you done missed on de reason. It's 'cause quality folks an poverty is strugglin' in dere together. Po white trash don't suffer no mo wid bein' po den you'd suffer up dere in dat cocoanut tree; 'cause dats all dey is use to an fittin' to do. Wid quality folks, dat 'mounts to somethin'; silk is natural but rags scratches."

They were both silent. Emma's eyes were on the Judge's window, and Eddie's on his empty plate from which he had just mopped the last vestige of red bean gravy. His appetite was an oft repeated compliment to Emma's culinary prowess, but one which she did not always appreciate. She was watching him furtively from time to time.

"Fo' Gawd sake, Eddie," she said

presently, with a toss of her head, "what make you take so powerful long? Ain't you thoo dat dog bait an puppy portion dat you put on yo' plate?"

"Yas mam, Aun' Emma, I done reach de bottom of it long ago, but I'm peckin' my teeths."

"Well, hurry up wid dat. Make it brief. I wants to git upstairs."

Eddie worked diligently with his tooth-pick. "You ain' goin' up dere to tell de boss I lef' you, is you?" he asked in a pleading voice.

Emma looked at him disdainfully and shook her head. "No indeed; I ain' goin' to take up de Jedge's time wid dat fool-ishmen'. You can't help bein' shiftless. No use me tryin' to moderate you. Gawd de onlies' man can keep you busy, an dat's why he gin you dem two sets o' upper teeths an dat fatal appetite; fo' you spens

mos' yo' time puttin' yo' teeth into somethin' an den takin' what's left out of em.''

Eddie's happiness, when he found he
was not going to be told on, was too great
to allow of any distress over the insults
that Emma was "tumblin' noble an shakin'
brief" over his head. His speed with the
toothpick diminished and, with a great
show of determination, he wrapped it
carefully in a piece of brown paper and
stuck it between the pot-shelf and the
wall.

"I'm ready now, Aun' Emma; signify
yo' erran'," he said cheerfully, wiping his
greasy hands on the roller towel hanging
on the back of the kitchen door.

The old negro woman smoothed her
checked gingham apron over her broad
knees and regarded him critically. After
all, he was scarcely more than a child and
she should not expect too much of him.

[42]

Her sympathetic understanding of the hearts of the white children she had nursed, and of her own "remaindin's of makin' up my baid wid a bohebious nigger" (as she described her offspring), gave her a deep knowledge of their psychology. Her oft-repeated receipt for good children was, "give em a sandrich of scolds an smiles"; and now, following her own advice to others, she was larding her ill humor with the pleasant banter that only the negroes know to perfection.

It was a great event for Eddie when he was allowed to sing hymns, and often when they suggested good old Baptist sentiments, Emma would join in and "make melody" than which there was nothing sweeter. When Eddie's memory failed him, his hymns broke down alarmingly in textual accuracy but his interpolations were picturesque and graphic.

From a more enlightened mentality they would have been blasphemous, but Eddie's fervor proved his sincerity, and Emma's reprimands were often his first realization that the hymn was not "as wrote down in de scripture."

Tonight, by way of being exceptionally indulgent, she let him sing his favorite and, with his round kinky head thrown back and his eyes shut, he chanted:

*"Go way back to de manger
An talk of corn an straw,
I'm de Lawd.
Go way back to de temple
An money-changers law,
I'm de Lawd.*

*"Go way back to de cross
An what de Marys saw,
An blieve in Jesus Christ
Or I'll sock you in de jaw,
I'm de Lawd."*

[44]

Eddie stopped to take breath and was starting on another verse when Emma interrupted him.

"Quit yo' triflin' wid dat hime! Don't you know Gawd patience goin' wear out on you some day? It bad 'nough to hear Methodis' himes if dey right, but when you sing em wrong, dat's as good as puttin' a *gris-gris* on yo' do'-step. You better jine us Baptis' church an come up wid de sinners. Dat's where you b'long."

"Dey got too much water in de Baptis' church to suit me, Aun' Emma," Eddie said sleepily. "I ain' got no callin' fo' de bottom o' de river an . . ."

But Emma had seen the light glimmering through the shutters of the Judge's window, and she made haste to lock up the kitchen so she could get upstairs and talk over her worries about the Ledoux family. She sent Eddie on his way home,

[45]

and as he closed the heavy iron gate behind him, he was gaily whistling a tune in
double notes; the two tones blending so
closely that they sounded as one; the negroes' peculiar trick of trilling every note
so as to produce an effect of soprano and
alto parts.

THE Judge was sitting in his large
leather chair before the bulging, shallow grate piled high with its oozing,
sputtering coals. It seemed to have thrown
out its smutty chest in an effort to blow
enough heat into that large high-ceilinged
room to make it comfortable for the bald-
headed man with his thin fringe of gray-
ing hair. On the table beside him was a
double-barreled lamp whose domed shade,
of white underneath and green on top,

[46]

had lived through the vicissitudes of many years with only a chip here or a small crack there to tell of its narrow escapes. It had become a dreaded superstition that the Judge would never read again if the shade got "smithered," so great care was taken of it, for he was the pivot of the household.

Hero-worshipers in the North generally selected a national character, but hero-worshipers in the South rarely went beyond their own front doors.

Judge Markham wasn't an old man in years but it was only his eyes that had stayed young. They sparkled and danced under their half-lowered lashes at the slightest excuse, but they could grow hard and glitter when, to use Emma's words, "right was wrecked an honesty tramped on."

He was fairly short and more than

fairly round, and his Prince Albert coat with its flapping tails never looked new nor pressed, no matter how new or pressed it really was. It had a way of settling to him that was inevitable. His trousers always appeared to wear their creases on the outside, and his black string tie was chronically coming undone.

He was a man of wide knowledge and his willingness to share it with anyone in need made him an intensely popular figure. Many a young lawyer, trying a case for the first time, gained confidence from his kindly smile and helpful suggestions and carried home with him a new conception of the meaning of "Judge."

He radiated the keenest human curiosity about every case that came before him and desired to know even the smallest details that had a bearing on it. There never was a prejudiced nor mind-shut ex-

pression on his pleasant face, and his asso-
ciates on the bench said that he *hoped*
more people innocent than he ever ad-
judged guilty. A perennial optimist, he
had borne greater disappointments than
is the common lot, yet they had never
soured him. The negroes in the neighborhood turned to him in every emergency.
Deaths, births, and going to law, they
made his especial concern, and they
brought their trivial disagreements to
him and accepted his decisions without
question or murmur.

On the night when Chief of Police
Hennessey was shot by some Italians because he threatened to expose the work-
ings of their secret society, and all sorts
of wild tales were running around back
of town among the negroes, the Judge
sat calmly on his front gallery, with his
double-barrelled shotgun on his knees,

guarding the entrance to his back yard. It was full of colored people who came from every direction, seeking his protection. At times their frenzied prayers and hymns became too loud for safety, so he went to the side gate and admonished them in no uncertain terms and returned again to his all-night vigil on the front porch.

Several small bands of noisy rioters poured up the street on the way to St. Charles Avenue, and many hapless negroes, in the path of their mob violence, suffered; but Judge Markham's flock gradually lapsed into a feeling of safety and slumber, and it was many days before the last of them left his protection for their homes. It was an anxious time in New Orleans and the events that followed brought about a break in diplomatic relations between America and Italy, but to the negroes it only meant that once again the "Jedge" had proved to be their best friend, and he became the "texes" for many a colored preacher's sermon. "Pertec' de meek an de lonely, de way Mister Jimmie done."

As Emma's knock was unanswered, she opened the door noiselessly and peeped in. The Judge was sleeping in his large leather chair before the fire. His face seemed worn and furrowed. It worried her. Never had he looked so old and sick. She caught her breath audibly.

"Great glory!" she ejaculated as he opened his eyes. "You certainly sont my heart on a long journey when I seen you lookin' so peaked an still. Why didn' you call me to bring you a strong toddy an a hot mustard feet bath? Ain't you know enough to lif' yo' voice out dat back winder an call Emma? What I been here fo', fo' de las' forty years, nursin' you an Miss Louise, an bornin' all dese chillun, if you can't notify me when dey got misadventure in de house?" She paused to take breath and was starting off again when the Judge held up his hand in mock supplication.

"Heaven forbid that I fail to call you the next time I feel sleepy," he said smilingly, but Emma was too worried by the sight of his tired worn face to be set aside so lightly.

"Sleepy! You worst den dat. You talkin' like Pompey dreamp," she went on, "dat buckeyes was biscuits an Muscovy ducks was stage-horses; but you can't fluzzle me. I knows you ain' feelin' peart. You jes all wore out; dats what it is. De firs' one o' dem lawyer-mens I ketch comin' in here lowratin' on dat Myrum Gaines case an askin' you to

straighten out dey sacrements, I'm goin'
thow em bodaciously out dat winder.
Dey wears you spindlin'."

The Judge burst out laughing.

"What I done said now to shake out yo'
chuckles?" Emma asked slowly, as Mrs.
Markham came to the door to see what all
the merriment was about.

"Oh, nothing—only, I don't straighten
out their sacraments; it's their *documents*
you mean."

Emma looked shame-faced, but the
Judge took no notice of it and went on.
"You should feel sorry for Myra Clarke
Gaines. Her case has been before the
courts a long time."

"Sho has. Reckon it started 'bout de
time de stars fell. Dat's de year I was
found in de ash-hopper. De lawyer-mens
will be scrabblin' over it till her las' two-
bits is gone, den her money an dey intrus

goes out hand in arm together. But what dat she want, anyhow?"

"She claims all of New Orleans, Emma, and says. . . ."

"All of Noo Orlyuns!" the old woman interrupted excitedly. "Why don't she pick herse'f out a small place like Gritny? What she want wid de whole Noo Lighted States?" She stood with her hands on her broad ample hips. "Seems to me when white-folks gets greedy it takes a lot to satisfy em; but I ain' comed up here to study 'bout anythin' escept my own troubles, an I'm seekin' counsel."

And then she told the Judge and Mrs. Markham all about her visits to the little gray cottage on Annunciation Street, and how the poor, sick lady had been sent to California, all alone.

She appreciated having such attentive listeners and told them every detail of her worry. It was cumulative, and the more she talked, the more her anxiety grew. How the two girls had gotten their mother to the street car was a mystery to her, which she did not fail to expatiate upon. Maybe the driver came over to help them, for the banquettes were slushy and full of bad places, but they didn't generally like to go so far away. At that time of day, if he wasn't sick, old George Barteau was driving the route, and he always helped everybody on and off the car and delivered packages and carried children across the street. His mule was trained to waiting and it seemed to prefer to stand still any time and rest itself and its bells. This was better than jangling along the uneven tracks, with a rattling car on its heels.

When George's errands detained him a long time, he started off his mule at a brisk trot to make up the lost minutes, and the old car with its flat wheels swung from side to side as though trembling with excitement over its own reckless speed.

She could see in her mind's eye the two girls sitting down on either side of their mother, trying to keep her warm in the draughty old car, and she was certain that George had to tap his bell many times before they remembered to drop their fares in the glass box behind him. At Jackson Avenue she knew they had to change cars, but that was easy; lots of people would be there, and sick-folks are *every*body's business in the South. The part of the journey she dwelt on the most tragically was the long block from the turn-table to the steamboat, and then the tiresome walk in Gretna.

"Why didn't they get a carriage? It's only two dollars for a whole hour," Mrs.

[56]

Markham said, with her quiet, placid drawl.

"Lawd knows, Ole Miss."

"Haven't you been giving them money in some way or other?"

"Yas mam. I been puttin' six-bits in de bunnels evvy time I goes, an I does dat startlin' reglar."

"You could have put a dollar in if you hadn't bought a lottery ticket each week."

"Who dat say I been takin' lottery tickets?" she questioned fiercely; "I wants to know who carryin' de nigger news to de white-folks."

Emma had promised the Judge, on many occasions, to stop her gambling habits and she was doing her best to put up a belligerent front that might discount the truth of the gossip just retailed to him. From his expression she knew she had failed. She was silent and confused.

Judge Markham looked at her fixedly and, as his eyes dropped to the floor at her feet, she glanced down apprehensively. There, sprawling on the yellow matting, were two crumpled pink lottery tickets that had spilled out of her overloaded pocket. There was no use denying what they were. No one in New Orleans could ever mistake them. Every waste-paper basket in the city knew them intimately. Her guilt was evident, so, to hide her embarrassment, she stooped down to pick them up, and smoothed them out on her knee.

"By rights, dis here can't be call playin' lottery. Dey jes some gig an saddle I dreamp out yistiddy night," she drawled in a half-tone.

Neither the Judge nor Mrs. Markham said a word. Their silence made Emma fidget uncomfortably in her chair. After a while she glanced up. "No use lookin' like grief in de cemetery. I knows I done broke my promise." And then she added hesitatingly: "So did Adam an Eva, but dey turned over a new leaf."

She laughed nervously. Folding the pink tickets carefully, she put them back in her yawning pocket and pinned the two gaping sides of it together with a huge safety-pin that generally anchored her little red shawl around her fat shoulders. Still no notice was taken of her. Judge Markham reached for his book. That was always the sign that he wished to be alone.

Emma got up from her chair stiffly. "Why don't you call me in my name befo' I go, Mister Jimmie?"

"No use, Emma; you know what you are without my telling you."

"Yas sir, I does, but I ain' as disappointed to find it out as you is."

[59]

"I am sorry to agree with you on that, but when an old friend deceives *me,* of course I am bitterly disappointed."

This was too much for the old colored woman, and large tears welled up in her eyes and sliding down her fat cheeks, lost themselves in the broad expanse of her blue-ginghamed bosom. She looked like the picture of woe as she stood staring listlessly into the fire, while tears and more tears chased each other down her face. A sudden resentment against the two pink lottery tickets seized her. Not only had they failed to win for her in the drawing, but now they had brought her this second batch of regrets, and this was *too* much. She was on the point of making another promise but thought better of it and turned toward the door.

"Going, Emma?" asked Mrs. Markham pleasantly.

"Yas mam; reckon I better. I got to find my can o' truth powder an put a tetch of it in my lef' shoe. Gawd knows I'm standin' in de need."

As she went out and said goodnight, she closed the door softly behind her and shuffled off down the long gallery that led to her room.

"Lawd A'mighty!" she said under her breath, as she looked back at the Judge's window through which the light gleamed brightly; "I sure was lucky dat only *two* of them damn things fell out."

Many days went by before Emma felt sufficiently reinstated in favor to brave the scrutinizing look in the Judge's eyes. Although she had dreamed numbers every night, she had not played the lottery once, and had the assurance of conscious virtue. Nothing makes so thick a shield. Thus armed, she decided to take "dat windin' stairs and dat ramblin' gallery" to the room above, where she knew Mrs. Markham would be sewing at the window.

She was a lovely lady of the pale shadowy type. During the long, hot summers she wore embroidered white mull gowns with Watteau pleats down the back. There were frosted pink buttons up to her chin, and her ashen hair was always piled high on her head. She could pay Emma no greater compliment than to change these dainty white gowns often; for "to wash an iron for Ole Miss" was as much a ritual as a joy to her. Emma would walk blocks to get a sprig of new cedar to rub her flat-iron on, and the smell of its scorched pungency was a sure indication that her most meticulous care was being expended. She usually sang over her tubs and ironing board, and from either a sense of fitness or need of spiritual encouragement, she unfailingly chose the good old Baptist hymn, *Washed in de Blood of de Lamb*.

She was not content to sing softly but was unconsciously anxious to have all the neighborhood know that she was at her devotions. Now that it was too cold to wash on the open back gallery, her Mondays were quieter and less enjoyable to her.

By way of making her entrance into "de white-folks distric' " an easy one, she had brought up a stack of the children's clothes done in her matchless style, the lace edgings fluted and all exuding the fresh, clean smell of warm vetiver.

Mrs. Markham wasn't sewing by the window as Emma expected she would be, but she was hunting among a lot of small bottles for one marked "Sweet Spirits of

Nitre," which Humphrey's Homeopathic Chart, tacked up in the nursery, indicated for slight fever. The children were restless and irritable and she thought possibly they needed medicine. One of the comforting things about homeopathy was that the dose of medicine given was so small that, if they didn't really need it, it didn't do them any harm.

Emma dreaded having Ole Miss get started on her "dosin's," for she would always arrange a row of glasses, a piece of paper covering each one, with a spoon on top, and most complicated directions as to alternate doses every fifteen minutes or some such interval of time. The children, with malicious delight, would mix the glasses up the moment Emma's back was turned; or drink them all at one gulp and keep her in constant terror for fear they would kill themselves; so that, when she saw "dat Humphrey look" in Mrs. Markham's eye, she decided to give up taking a basket to Alys, as she had planned, but to send Eddie with it instead.

"I ain' seen dat bottle since a long time. Lever you min' lookin' for it. I'll tend de chillun dis evenin'. If dey needs medicine I'll acquaint you."

There was a loud shout from the nursery as Emma went in. She soothed and scolded and told war-time stories about the surrender of Vicksburg, which she remembered vividly, if inaccurately. What if she *did* embroider and enlarge some of the facts and ignore others? More erudite historians do as much. She was a born story-teller, so, after all, she was true to her avocation.

When she had all the children fast asleep, she crept out of the room noiselessly and went down to the kitchen to wait for Eddie to come back from his errand to the Ledoux house on Annunciation Street. She had sent him with a loaf of "chittlin' bread" and a paper plate piled high with *grillades* and rice, and she was anxious to know if it got there safely. She hadn't long to wait.

He came in, breathless. His tale of passing the corner where the arc lights sputtered, and walking over an immense circle of dead beetles—those large, gray, hard-backed, nippered bugs that were brought into New Orleans on the banana boats from Central America—and how they crunched and snapped as he ran over them, amused Emma and she chuckled merrily. Eddie's eyes were large with fright and stood out from his black face like two white buttons. It had evidently been a hard trip for him, and that he went at all spoke well for Emma's discipline.

After the day he had left her without warning, he had "walked careful an stepped light" to get on the right side of her again.

"Yas mam, I'm tellin' you what Gawd loves, an dat's de truth," he said breathlessly. "Dat gate sho shuck itself. I jes rested my han' on it an it rattle like a pair o' bones."

"Sure it rattle. Boy, you jes naturally was so skeered dat yo' han' trimbled; but I ain' studyin' 'bout dat. I wants to know did my victuals traverse safe, an who did you see?"

"It was de tall young lady; all wrap up jes like de las' time I seen her—even to de gloves. She comed out from de back wid a lamp in her han'. If it hadn' been for dat I couldn' tole she was comin' a-tall, drape up in dem black clothes like a hearse."

Emma stopped him with a gesture. "Don't you wrestle off de middle o' de road wid yo' conversation," she commanded. "I ain' payin' no never min' to *what* you think 'bout de way she keep de col' from searchin' roun' her person."

Eddie took his rebuke in silence and went on with his story, delivering the messages "de tall young lady" sent.

"Didn' you tell her what kep' me way, an dat my han' got out on chittlin' bread, an dat. . . ."

But Eddie confessed he had not wasted any time on useless conversation. If Emma had known the truth, he could not have spent *less* time and gone at all. Every step he took on the old brick banquette crackled as if he were walking on paper, and every house he passed was lightless and noiseless. Cold weather did away with passive leisure and set every one at the active task of keeping warm; hard to accomplish in those small frame houses built in the shape of a sleeping camel; low in front, rising to a second story in the back, and tapering off with sheds more or less innumerable, filled with wash-tubs, fat pine, charcoal and soft coal. Some one in New Orleans should erect a statue to the first miner of that priceless commodity, for *all* the inhabitants of that lovely city have warmed their shins at its smutty blaze, from infancy to maturity and old age.

Generally the streets were full of children playing and laughing, but not to-night. Eddie was alone as he stumbled along the uneven sidewalk: no other person in sight as he peered up and down. His courage throve best in daylight and company; now it had gone into total eclipse. He became afraid of the noise

of his own footsteps, so he tiptoed quietly
as he came up to the square-topped gate.
The *grillades* were trickling out of the
lagniappe plate. The feeling of the warm
grease on his hand was not unpleasant,
except that it reminded him of Emma.
Her rage would be terrible if she knew
he had gotten her contributions all "druz-
zlin'." Levelling up his package, he laid
his hand on the gate just as a light moved
slowly around in the back yard, behind
the thick gray branches of the old trumpet
vine. Eddie saw it stop and he felt that
some one was looking at him. Somehow
he could not hold his hand still, and the
warm gravy bathed his cold fingers.

"My legs tol' me to go, but my min' tol'
me to stay." It had been a tough struggle
but he had won out, and like many another
hero, he didn't want to be called upon to
repeat his act of heroism.

"Aun' Emma, I wants to talk *noble* wid you now; I wants to talk solemn. Please, mam, don' put me thoo dat tribulation agin. I ain' been much good 'bout waitin' on de table. . . ."

"You sho ain't."

"Well, I can improve. I ain' been swif' 'bout bringin' up dem fatal buckets o' coal. . . ."

"Now you tellin' what Gawd loves!"

"But I can improve. I ain' been previous 'bout finishin' up in de evenin'. . . ."

"It's yo' teeths what keeps you."

"I'll leave off peckin' em no mo, if you promise not to ast me to go roun' yonder agin."

Emma was sorry for the boy, who had gone gray with fright. He tried her patience at times, but she had grown fond of him; and then, too, his wholesale promise to better his behavior should be encouraged; so she agreed, in the future, to go herself to the dreary little cottage and never to send him alone again.

They sat in silence for a long time, Eddie becoming calmer and Emma nodding. After awhile Emma definitely came to the end of her nap.

"Eddie," she said meditatively, "I been studyin' 'bout yo' declarations, an I say here an now, you got to keep dat promise o' waitin' at de table better an bringin' up de coal buckets faster. Dats natural for a do-right boy, an nobody goin' 'spute you; but as for dat las' promise 'bout peckin' yo' teeths: I better loose you from dat, 'cause how is you goin' tetch up on yo' speed when you got all dat good-tastin' victuals tucked up in yo' teeths, takin' yo' mind off yo' business?"

WITH the coming of spring New Orleans shook herself free of the sickness and depression the unusual winter had forced upon her. The first new leaves of the camphor trees seemed an encouragement to other green things, and soon the wistarias draped trellises and fences with their bunches of lavender and purple gauze. The tiny white star blossoms of the Confederate jasmine against the background of its shiny dark leaves added its perfume to the sweet olive, whose delicacy and wonder of scent has never truly been caught by any perfumer. The cry-baby trees hung themselves with clusters of their noisy blooms, like coral lanterns threading through their branches, and the crêpe-myrtles, those marvels of incomparable beauty, completely covered themselves with showers of pink or white crinkled confetti in such prodigality, that only their trunks were visible under the glory of their tissue-like flowers.

Nothing can be more bewildering than a New Orleans spring and summer, and nothing more difficult to describe; for there are so many little flowers that add their beauty of color and perfume to the seductive loveliness of the whole; so many droning bees and fluttering butterflies; so many red-throated lizards that preen themselves on sunny board fences; so many darting insects of every hue, and, framing all this bounty are the large, far-branched live-oak trees where mocking-birds sing and sparrows chatter.

Negro nursemaids with their white charges dot the streets everywhere, and the gay-colored dresses and ribbons of the women, and the white and blue linen clothes of the men, give New Orleans the appearance of a huge garden party with ice cream wagons on the side streets and balloon-men and organ-grinders at every corner: a brilliant kaleidoscope of constantly changing beauty.

Into this gay riot of color and life a funeral procession wended its way. Two black horses, covered with fly-swishers knotted in large squares and finished along the bottom with black tassels, drew the shiny hearse. At each of its four corners stiff varnished plumes stood up like minarets. The driver's stove-pipe hat was less glistening, but the tears that ran down his black face were picked out by the sunshine and challenged the sparkle of the silver handles on the coffin inside. His grief was elemental and unashamed.

The Judge was dead. All that was left of him was being followed to the grave by a long queue of carriages of every kind

[75]

and vintage, and wagons in varying states of more or less dilapidation.

At the end of the line of these slow moving vehicles there trudged a solitary figure, her awkward, ponderous body in a black calico dress and her head tied up in a black handkerchief. The by-standers gasped as they recognized Emma. Had she been forgotten and left behind by mistake?

As she toiled along the dusty road, a gentleman on the banquette asked a colored girl who she was.

"Dats Jedge Markham ole mammy what nursed him."

In a second he had crossed the gutter and, with his hat in his hand, asked Emma if he could drive her to the graveyard.

The tears were running down the furrows in her kind old face, but she answered in a low steady voice as she shook

[76]

her head: "Thank you, sir. I could a-went wid de family, but I got to walk. I got to carry my cross to Calvary."

AFTER Dr. Speed, the Judge's closest friend, had gone through his papers, it was found that very little was left for his wife and children, except some small life insurance policies. The same old Southern story was being told again: an indulgent father, a business-ignorant mother, and children whose only knowledge of money was its equivalent in pralines, stage-plank gingerbreads and Meissonier's ice cream.

It is well that the grandeur and meaning of real friendship, its unselfishness, its promptness, its religion of personal service, has never been more completely told anywhere than in New Orleans; for it is there most seriously needed. Financial disaster leaves the social status unchanged and favors do not come as charity, but as homage to courageous bearers of sorrow.

Nowhere are women, born to huge plantations, myriad servants and seemingly unlimited pocketbooks, braver in the face of a sudden, total collapse of their old world. The boarding-houses bore mute witness in the superlative degree, for most of them were run by the impoverished gentlewomen whose only money-making talent was housekeeping. It was this way that calamity was met with the poise and dignity inherent to their breeding.

Poverty was nothing to be ashamed of. So many of one's friends suffered from the same disease; and, after all, it was superficial, since the sons were educated and grew up into their father's clubs, and

[78]

the daughters made their débuts just the same. Organdy dresses and leghorn hats did not cost much, but they were all the girls needed to set off their soft beauty. In time, many of them married into an affluence they had never known, but to which, paradoxically, they seemed thoroughly accustomed. Perhaps this came, quite naturally, from their total indifference to money, since wealth, per se, had never been necessary to their enjoyment.

A few weeks after Judge Markham's death, when all the assets of his estate had been definitely estimated, it was plainly evident that there was no way to keep the old house, educate the children and pay the servants, except by taking in "paying guests." After much discussion it was agreed upon and Emma began arranging things. Old pieces of furniture were brought in from the storage space over

[79]

the stable, to replace those of particular association which were moved into "Ole Miss room."

Little by little an air of impersonality settled over everything, and Emma surveyed her work with approval as she moved about the spare room which she was getting ready for occupancy.

Dr. Speed's old bachelor brother with courtly manners and dyspepsia, was coming to take up his abode in a few days and the whole household was awaiting his arrival with secret alarm. The children had been cautioned about noises "outen yo' own precinc'," and Eddie had been told not to "ramble so heavy when dat bad stomach comes here wid his genal discontent."

Before she closed the door to the room for the first paying guest, she gave a last pat to the mosquito-bar that hung from the blue tester on the large walnut bed, and shuffled up the hall noiselessly, stopping outside "Ole Miss" door to wreathe her face in smiles like a prima donna ready to make her entrance on the stage. There was no mawkish sentimentality about Emma, nor Pollyanna simper; but she believed in dealing hands to people that they could play and, within her circumscribed limits, she protected those she cared for with the fierce intensity of her Indian-African forebears.

Mrs. Markham had just settled herself by the window, with a book in her hand, when Emma peeped in.

"I didn' knock fo' fear you was crumblin' into a nap."

"Just finished one," smiled Mrs. Markham, "and now I'll read a bit before the children come home from school. Have you finished everything? . . ." She hesitated and pointed in the direction of the room at the end of the hall.

"Yas mam," Emma answered gaily, "an I'm mighty glad we got a single genelman. He be good for us all."

"Why Emma! What do you mean? I thought you minded having strangers about."

"Whosomever tol' you dat is hasslin' wid de truth. Dat genelman guest goin' better us all. Dese chillun been wil' lately wid dey loud talkin' an boisterous ways."

"I haven't noticed that."

"Yas mam. An Eddie is tramplin' like a passel o' cotton mules all over de lot."

"That's strange. I haven't heard him, and I generally have such keen ears."

"*Yas* mam," Emma went on breathlessly, "an I gone shiftless on light bread an hot rolls. . . ."

"But, Emma, you mustn't give Mr.

Speed those things. He has dyspepsia."

"Lever min', he can *look* at em; an anyway, we is lucky to have a bachler-genelman wid no peevish lady pokin' 'bout."

"Why, you big humbug! You always said bachelors were like mint-juleps with the brandy left out."

"I was talkin' random then, Ole Miss; —but lemme get out o' here, 'cause dem chillun be comin' home pretty quick now, an I got to git em all ready for Sunday school in de mornin'." And she beat a hasty retreat before she struck her colors.

THE children's attendance at Sunday school was the culmination of unceasing effort begun early Saturday afternoon when their clothes were laid out, stiff-starched and ruffled, fresh from Emma's careful iron and the big wooden wash-tub placed before the grate fire for their weekly scrubbing. It was the time of alluring story-telling on Emma's part, and of shivering reluctance on the children's, which increased, with cold weather, to open rebellion. Somehow or other the results were accomplished, however, and the children and Emma, conscious of their Sunday grandeur, would walk up the brick banquette to the church on the corner, just as the last stroke of the bell died away.

In summer Emma would sit on the steps while her charges were taught to "wrestle wid de word o' Gawd," but in winter time she came into the Sunday school room to sit by the stove and listen to the "skimp Christianity dat white-folks teaches chillun."

Sometimes she'd try to strengthen their knowledge of the Bible by telling them *her* versions, and her description of the founding of her race was a favorite bribe. With its help she accomplished many difficult tasks with tangled hair and loose teeth.

This is the way she told it:

"Once, when it want quite day, an de Lawd hadn' got thoo layin' out de banquettes an pastin' up de stars an tinselin' de moon, he seen three onery mens shufflin' 'long de road. Dey was all different sizes an talkin' serious 'bout what was dey chances to git famblies an be forefathers, when dey comed up to a wide gutter full o' muddy water, an no tellin' how deep it was. It laid clear cross dey path an o' course dey had to res' an talk it over, jes like mens will do.

"Well, after dey done tackle de ques-

tion from all sides an got deyse'f all riled-
up 'bout who could jump over de bes', dey
heard a dreadful rookus in de sky, an de
Lawd thowed open his shetters an leaned
out, an he says, 'Look here, boys! You
raisin' a mighty commotion; shakin' all my
rivets loose, an I don't see no reason fo' it,
neither. Can't you be patienable an arger
gentle till de world settles solid?'

"At dat, dey all three started splainin'
at once dat it was de udder feller what
make de mos' noise; but de Lawd shushed
em, an looked angry-like an wrinkled up
his forehead under his heavy gold crown.
De mens got skeered an listened to his
words, an he say: 'Dat ditch done laid it-
se'f dere purposeful an providential.
You all been lowratin' 'bout forefatherin'
an you wants to start a fambly of yo' *own*,
so you each another mus' git yo'se'f a race
seprate. Dis world need to be full o' dif-

ferent colors o' people; 'cause if de famblies is all alike dey won't have nobody to
talk 'bout an dey couldn' be happy; so I
got to 'range it so *talkin'* goin' be de spe-
cial job of *evvybody,* an I'm goin' have
nations of different colors an different
creeds.'

"De Lawd stop to clare his thoat an
went on: 'Now you three argerfiers git
back dere an taw to de line, an when you
all jumps dat gutter, I'm goin' give you
each one a race for yo' own dat you can
be de forefather to. Dere won't be no
swappin' o' titles neither, if you don't like
yo' denomination, for what I says stands.
I'm goin' mark you wid yo' nation, an
whosomever tries to change hisse'f into
somethin' else, will be worse den a suck-
egg hound wid no frien's or comp'ny nowhere. So stan' up for yo' kind what's
natural to you an stick by yo' people, no

matter how you disrespecs em. Now take yo' places an come 'cordin' to size.'

"And den de Lawd rested hisse'f for a little while.

"Well, chillun, dem mens lined up somethin' *noble* an *speedy,* 'cause mens always likes to start somethin'. When de Lawd seen dey was ready, he slap his hands loud an de firs' man got a good start an he give a mighty jump an landed clare cross on de other side, on dry groun', an de Lawd said: 'You is sho active an got keen eyes an can see in de future, so I'm goin' make you father of de white race.'

"De nex' feller tried powerful, but he want so rangey an his eyes was slanched, so he couldn' gage hisse'f an he landed on de edge o' de puddle an got all spatterated wid dirty water, an de Lawd was peeve an he say: 'Maybe you never is goin' be any bigger an you always got to see things bias 'cause o' de way yo' eye-hole is cut; so I'm goin' make you de Pa o' de yaller race.'

"Somethin' tuck up de Lawd attention right den, an he jugged his head in his winder an was busy inside, so he want lookin' when de las' man jumped. Dat little feller was *butt*-headed an had number twelve flat feets dat done lost dere spring, so when he jump de bes' he could, bless Gawd! he landed *plunk* right in de middle o' de gutter an was all kivvered with mud.

"When de Lawd turn roun' an look at him, he was a-standin' dere laughin' hisse'f to death, wid only his teeths an de whites o' his eyes a-showin'. De more he laugh de more he roll his big eyes, an de more he roll his big eyes de more de Lawd laugh an shake his shoulders. An den de white race jined in de laugh, and de yaller race laugh, an den de whole world was a-rockin'; an all of a sudden it come bright day, an de Lawd say: 'I names you Sambo—an you is de forefather of de black race. An jes to show dey ain' no hard feelin's twixen us, I'm goin' give you bountiful laughter an singin' over *all* de other races.'

"An dat's why de colored folks is so happy; an de thunder you chillun hears evvy now an den, is jes de ole echo of dat first laughin'; and de *sun*shine is jes de glistnin' of Sambo teeths when he was kivvered up wid mud, a-grinnin' at de Lawd, in de puddle."

EVERY Sunday afternoon found Emma completely tuckered out. Her mid-day dinner was always a triumph of quality and quantity and, since this was the last one the little family would enjoy alone, she "double-determined" to have it her best.

She arranged the centerpiece of sweet olive and lantana, and "drugged out" all the company linen and silver, and had ambrosia for dessert.

"I done put my bes' foot forred so many times dat I jes naturally thowed it out o' joint," she said meditatively, as she surveyed the pot of savory gumbo, the great pan of crisp rolls and the marshmallow cake, each waiting its turn to be served up in honor of the memory of days past, before the guests were paying ones.

Emma asked Mrs. Markham to say the blessing, but "Ole Miss" was too full of emotion to trust her voice. If it trembled, the children's mirth at Emma's surprise would be shadowed, so she smiled softly and shook her head. There was an awkward pause. The children looked at each other. Suddenly, the little boy bowed over the table, his light curls falling into his plate, and in a low, solemn voice, repeated the blessing he had heard his father say so many times.

It was a gay feast and one that would have turned scientific dietitians into gibbering idiots, but it served its purpose and left a bright shining spot in the memory of those who shared it.

Emma had not been to the cottage on Annunciation Street since the sudden death of Judge Markham and it had preyed on her mind constantly; but there was so much to do at home, her days didn't seem long enough to accomplish it all.

Her old legs were getting stiffer, her old back getting rounder, and she suffered with "twinkles of pain here an dere," so it was more and more difficult for her to finish up her work, mind the children and cheer up "Ole Miss"; but today "bein' Sunday an my las' free time befo' dat Eva searchin' bachler-genelman comes up here wid his raw stomach an his cooked conscience," she decided to fill her basket and go.

"Why, Emma, you're too tired. You should sit down and rest awhile. Send Eddie with your basket," urged Mrs. Markham.

"I can't sen' him. He ain' no good as a consolement offerin'. I better go *myse'f*. Somethin' is workin' on my min'. It's been tellin' me to go all day, an now it's repeatin' rapid."

"For Heaven's sake! If you feel that way about it, don't stop to multiply words but go at once. What would you do if something was really wrong? You haven't any money, have you?"

"Only two-bits; but I done tol' Doctor Speed all about it, an he promised to stan' by me financial. Don't worry yo'se'f, Ole Miss, while I'm gone; for you know you kin sure spin a reckless tale wid yo' 'magination; so if you set peaceful ginst I gets back, I'll tell you *zactly* how I finds things in dat lonesome sorrow nes' over yonder."

Emma's getting downstairs safely always depended upon the strength of the banister, for she leaned against it with all her weight as she shuffled her unwieldy body and flat feet down one step after another. On level ground she made fairly good speed but her progress was accompanied by a switching of her full starched skirts that gave her the grotesque appearance of a giant top sidling up the street.

[94]

When she reached the corner of Harmony near the gloomy cottage, she shivered unpleasantly. "Ugh!" she grunted, "dat sure was a mule-size rabbit dat cross my grave swif'. Wonder why he pick out *dis* time to lope over my bones?"

With determination she rattled the square wooden gate. It sounded hollow and empty. She waited a moment then rattled it again. No stir at the shutters or in the back yard. Again she shook it noisily. She waited a moment, tense with listening, then wheeled around clumsily and started down the street toward Dr. Speed's house, as though possessed.

When she reached it she was breathless, and perspiration was running off her face in a steady stream and losing itself on her broad panting bosom.

The doctor was making out his bills laboriously and with fine Spencerian flourishes, as though only by æsthetic beauty would they gain immediate attention. Emma's face, as she burst open the door, alarmed him.

"Mrs. Markham?" he asked hurriedly, reaching for his black bag, without which no homeopathic doctor could, in those days, properly diagnose a case.

Emma shook her head. She was nearly spent. "It's Alys, dat little chile," she managed to say.

"Is she sick? Have you seen her?"

"Seen *nobody*. Ain' *nobody* come to de gate."

Why worry then? She's probably out."

But Emma was starting down the walk toward the banquette, at a reckless gait, her flat feet padding the uneven bricks.

"Come back here! Wait a minute!" the doctor ordered sharply, as he grabbed his

[96]

hat and shut the door. "Get in my buggy, if you must go. It's the quickest way to get there."

He unhooked the snap on the horse's bit at the hitching post and picked up the reins. It was all he could do to push and pull Emma in, and he was not quite sure she wouldn't roll out as he turned the corner, so he grabbed her arm with his free hand.

The sudden stop in front of the cottage helped her to get to her feet and she half scrambled, half fell to the banquette, as Dr. Speed called hurriedly to the neighbors next door, for news of Alys and her sister.

They were slow-witted, apathetic people from the back parishes, and had lived there only a short while. They said they had never seen but *one* girl, and she had not been around for a week; they hadn't even seen a light in the house and thought maybe she'd gone away.

The doctor was inclined to be annoyed because Emma had broken up his Sunday afternoon for a wild goose chase, and he looked at her petulantly.

"Ain't you goin' do nothin'?" she urged with tears in her eyes.

"I can't break into a private house, no matter how much you want me to, that's a jail offense."

Emma appeared not to have heard him. She was rattling the gate frantically. With a great lunge, she threw her whole weight against it. The rusty screws pulled out of the old iron lock and it fell to the walk with a noisy clatter.

As the gate flew open they distinctly heard a faint cry. It seemed to come from the back yard somewhere. The doctor ran around the side of the house. As he passed a shuttered window a sickly-sweet odor stopped him short.

"You stay out of here!" he called back to Emma peremptorily. But it would have taken a battering ram to have made any impression upon her. With her head down and her arms swinging at her sides, she was making her top speed to catch up with him.

At a glance he could tell there was no one in the tiny yard, so he took the back steps at a jump, and tried the door. It was locked. He listened a moment. He could hear some one crying. It was thin and weak and sounded like a very young child.

Still the sickish, sweet odor persisted. It seemed to come from everywhere. It was almost overpowering.

Emma was on the porch now, ashen and breathless. "What you waitin' fo'?" she panted angrily. "Fo' me to bus' dis too?"

But before she had finished her sentence the doctor had shattered one of the flimsy panels in the door and, putting his hand through, shot back the bolt.

The stench was solid. They could almost see it. Again Dr. Speed ordered Emma to go home, but she paid no attention to him.

The room they entered was in half-darkness; no object was distinct in outline. There was a long-legged, iron wood stove on one side and, in the corner, a small cot. A tiny figure was on it, huddled under a brown cover that was ragged and torn and stained indescribably. It was Alys; aged and wizened and whiter than anything human.

The air was nauseating with the heavy odor of a horrible living death.

Emma could hardly recognize the pathetic creature who was trying to hide her face with her claw-like hands and shaking with dry, tearless whimpers.

"You ain' feared o' me, Alys? Dis is de doctor man an we done come to help you," she said soothingly, as she crossed the dirty, bare room.

Dr. Speed had taken some bottles from his bag and was mixing some milky liquids. He touched Emma's arm and shook his head, but she had already sensed that the child was dying. . . . How could her sister leave her alone like this? Surely she must be somewhere in the house. . . . Emma bent over the poor little girl. "Where yo' sister? Ain't she been tendin' you mos' as she could?"

"She's gone."

"Gone? Where she gone, chile?"

"To California . . . to mother." It ended almost in a whisper.

The doctor was trying to give her some medicine but she couldn't swallow it.

"Why *didn'* you sen' for me?" wailed Emma hopelessly, tears running down her cheeks.

"No use," came the queer, hollow voice, husky and deep and old. "I'm going to California now, too."

A few light gasps and a smile, and it was over.

WHAT she done had, Doctor?" sobbed Emma as she looked down at the gaunt, still figure on the dirty cot.

"Leprosy." And then he added in a lower tone, "Starvation."

"O Gawd!" Emma cried, her voice strident in prayer as she covered her face with her hands. "If I didn' think you knowed yo' business better den me I'd say you slip up now. Why you sen' all dis double trouble to a po little chile, when you could a-drabble it roun' on some o' yo' own age?"

She was down on her knees, rocking from side to side. "I'm gittin' *ole* an I ain' so strong as I was, but I could a-took some o' dat misery. An, O Lawd, answer dis question: why you sen' me dat spell o' crinklin' rheumatism? When you must a-knowed I ought to been here. What for you get mix up dat way when you generally works so systematic?"

Dr. Speed went over to Emma and helped her up. "Come now, mammy," he said gently, "that little girl is better off dead—but she *did* have a rotten deal."

"She sure did; an I never is to git over my part in dis till Jedgemen' Day. I'm *al*ways goin' pull dat starvation load, fo' my ole wagon ain' never goin' be empty of it."

The doctor led the weeping old colored woman out on the back gallery to get a breath of fresh air, but the thick stench seemed to follow them like a dog at their heels.

Suddenly they noticed several loose boards in the floor, which seemed carelessly tumbled together by someone in haste. Emma pushed them aside, and there in the soft earth underneath, they saw two graves with a blue china tureen between them, full of faded flowers.

Emma shook her head sorrowfully. "Dat must a-been her California," she said in a husky voice. "Dose Creoles make nobody dey confidence."